JOSHUA JAMES

JOSHUA JAMES

Richard A. Boning

Illustrated by

Gordon Johnson

The Incredible Series

Dexter & Westbrook, Ltd., Baldwin, New York

Printed in the United States of America

International Standard Book Number: 0-87966-104-6

To the
Hull Historical Society
Hull, Massachusetts

It was strange, folks said, how Joshua James began his battle with the sea. They knew that he was doomed to lose because the sea is stronger than any person — certainly stronger than a ten-year-old boy. But Joshua was Yankee-born and Yankee-stubborn, so the folks of Hull, Massachusetts, shrugged and held their tongues. They all knew that sooner or later the sea would claim him.

Not that Joshua didn't have cause, mind you. He did! It had all started on April 3, 1837, when his mother and baby sister sailed to Boston on the schooner *Hepzibah*. As the family waited for them to return, a neighbor brought the shocking news. The *Hepzibah* had gone down in the Hull Gut. Everyone aboard — lost.

There were tears in the James household that day. Captain James — hard as granite — wept. Young Joshua was dry-eyed and silent, a strange, set look on his face. The older folks fell silent and were uneasy when they saw his expression. His first words to his father were, "Teach me all you can about the sea."

Then folks realized what Joshua had in mind, and their blood chilled. Somehow he was going to make the sea pay a terrible price for the loss he had suffered.

Captain James' weather-beaten face whitened, but he smiled kindly at his son. "If that's your wish — but you must learn to live *with* the sea, not *against* it. Forget revenge."

It was then that Joshua took the oath that made old seafarers sweat and squirm. "If the sea ever tries to take anyone's life while I'm around, it'll have to take me first," he vowed. His father's heart tightened.

Neighbors gasped when they heard this defiance. They knew that Joshua's days were numbered, but they did have to admire how coolly he prepared himself for the battle he could not win.

Joshua went to sea almost daily with his father and older brothers. At first they argued with him. "Forget your vow," they said. But Joshua was *uncommon* stubborn. They took him along, and in time he began to demonstrate strange, almost uncanny abilities. For instance, they found that he could steer a boat accurately in heavy fog. Folks whispered about his strange talents.

Joshua explained, "The water talks to me." With his well-trained ear he could understand the language of the ocean.

His other powers could not be explained. Even far out at sea, where there was neither surf nor reef to guide him, Joshua always knew exactly where he was. One night it appeared he had lost his way. Glancing at the stars, Joshua predicted, "We'll raise a light inside of two hours." His father stared at him in disbelief — but in one hour and fifty-five minutes the light appeared!

Joshua had his first skirmish with the sea when he was fifteen. A boat set out to rescue the crew of a ship wrecked at Harding's Ledge. Wind and rain made it difficult to see. No one could even be sure who the rowers were.

After the rescue the captain was surprised to find that Joshua had sneaked in among the crew. "He pulled his oar as well as any sailor," marveled the skipper.

Everyone knew then that nothing would do until Joshua had his own boat. Then he could begin his battle with the sea in earnest.

On December 1, 1885, one of the worst storms in history staggered the New England coast. Off Nantasket Beach the lights of a brig, the *Anita Owen*, could barely be seen. A distress light glimmered. Unable to reach the safety of Boston Harbor, the ship could be saved only by a miracle.

"Can we reach it, Cap'n Joshua?" a sailor bellowed.

Joshua, now full-grown and in the prime of his career, was strong and full of purpose — a completely dedicated man. Squinting into the gloom, he could just barely make out the lights of the vessel about 300 yards off shore.

"It won't stay afloat long!" he shouted.

To the surprise of the few shivering townspeople huddled on the beach, Joshua ordered a lifeboat launched. Waves as high as twelve feet raced over the sea. A plunge into those icy waters meant certain death.

A seasoned mariner stepped forward from among the townspeople. "There isn't a person in New England who can put a boat out to that ship. Bravery is one thing, but why throw lives away?"

Joshua paid no heed. He took the steering oar. The lifeboat pulled away and knifed into the angry sea. It trembled on the crests of huge combers — then shot into the valleys between them. At times it disappeared under the foaming billows.

The shore was soon lost to view, but the lights of the *Anita Owen* were now clearly visible. A giant roller crashed over boat and crew.

"We're going under!" yelled a sailor.

Captain James calmly ordered two of the rescuers to bail. The boat remained afloat, but progress was impossible.

Though the crew pulled heroically, the lights of the *Anita Owen* gradually faded. Giant waves slowly forced the lifeboat back to the shore.

To the amazement of those on land, Joshua ordered the rescue crew to launch again. This time they successfully beat their way to the stricken ship. As they came close, a voice was heard above the gale. It was the captain of the *Anita Owen*.

"My wife and nine others aboard!"

As the giant waves pounded the lifeboat, Joshua made a quick decision. "We'll take five each trip!" he shouted.

As the lifeboat crept closer to the *Anita Owen*, Captain James directed the crew to lower one person at a time. "I'll signal when!" he roared into the wind.

The situation demanded precise timing. The lifeboat would first have to come under the vessel without being crushed — and then dart out again. Joshua tried and failed. The second time he was successful. The first to be rescued was the captain's wife.

Then, with the sea battering them toward land, the boat shot ahead. Once again they were flooded as a giant wave broke. Fortunately, the same wave drove the boat high up on the sand.

Joshua and his crew made the second trip. This time it was even more perilous. Spars and timber from the *Anita Owen* were churning in the water. Any one of them could sink the lifeboat in an instant. Coolly maneuvering among these dangerous obstacles, Joshua picked up the remaining five survivors.

As the boat emerged from the blackness, the townspeople stared in disbelief. Joshua and the crew were aglow — surrounded by a strange eerie light!

"It's the spray — froze on their coats," explained a veteran mariner. The townspeople murmured in awe.

Later, sailors drank deep from their mugs of rum.
"He won — this time." The meaning was clear to all.

As the years passed, Joshua continued to battle the waters, forcing the sea to give up its prey. Some folks said the ocean had met its match. But old-timers knew the sea still had a trick or two up its sleeve. They nodded wisely when they learned that the water was about to claim a ship while Joshua was far inland.

When word reached Joshua, he promptly asked, "Where's it settling?"

"Five hundred yards off shore, but it's three long miles by land before we can even launch," came the answer.

It appeared that the sea was at last to take a ship from Joshua. He had other ideas. He and his crew flagged down a train from Boston and roared down the coast.

The ship was the British schooner *Ulrica*, already going down. Was Joshua too late? So it seemed. Waves swept its decks and had forced the crew high into the rigging.

"Into the water," ordered Joshua, wasting no time.

Twice the raging waves slammed the rescuers back to shore. Just as they had finally managed to fight their way out to the *Ulrica,* the angry sea threw a giant wave directly at Joshua himself. It tore the steering oar from his hands, hurled him into the ocean, picked up the lifeboat as if it were a toy, and swept it back over his head. The roaring water seemed to be laughing at him — mocking him scornfully.

The idea maddened Joshua! He reached out, grasped an oar, and clung to it grimly as his boat was again swept back toward the beach.

"Bring up a Hunt gun!" he roared. "We'll shoot the ship a rope and rig a breeches buoy." Joshua aimed carefully and fired. His aim was true, but the sailors on the *Ulrica* were too weak to set up the buoy. The wind howled with fiendish glee, joining the sea in its war against Joshua!

A less dedicated person than Joshua James would have given up, but the persistent Yankee captain merely ordered the boat launched again.

"Don't row!" he shouted above the wind. "Pull yourselves and the boat along the rope."

Once again Joshua and his crew filled the boat with survivors. Once again he had outwitted the sea.

Now the elements had tired of their games with Joshua. On November 25, 1888, the sea lathered up a storm so big that it reached all the way from Maine to the Carolinas. Joshua woke up that morning sensing that something special was about to happen. With a few of his crew he battled his way up Telegraph Hill through lashing snow and wind. There were several schooners off Boston Light.

"It's bad, Cap'n — real bad!" his crew shouted. "We might reach one or two before they go down."

They all knew that no rescue attempt was possible until the ships lost anchor and were driven closer.

Joshua hurled defiance into the teeth of the storm. "We'll save all of them!" It seemed that the elements raged even more furiously, accepting his challenge.

Folks would talk about that storm for years to come. The wind was so strong that Joshua and his crew had to bend over double to walk, and shout into each other's ears to be heard. They had no choice but to wait for the ships to draw closer.

By two o'clock the *Cox and Green,* the first of the ships, had broken loose from its moorings. It was piled up on the rocks — ready to break apart.

Joshua called for the Hunt gun. Was there time? He knew he couldn't afford to miss. Squinting down the barrel, he fired. His aim was true. The wind screamed its disappointment as Joshua brought all nine sailors to safety.

Throughout that long afternoon Joshua and his crew paced the beach, waiting for another vessel to draw near. Finally, as it grew dark, a second ship was torn loose — the *Gertrude Abbott*.

The sea had flung it up on some rocks beyond reach of the Hunt gun. Waves were even higher than before. "We'll launch a boat," Joshua said. "Chances are it won't return. I'll command no one to go."

With that he leaped into the boat and grabbed the steering oar. His entire crew followed — and rowed as they had never rowed before.

Again and again the sea tried to batter the small craft against the stricken *Gertrude Abbott*, but Joshua was too quick. Each time he darted under the bow, a survivor was taken into the lifeboat. Eight attempts were made and eight people were taken aboard.

The townspeople of Hull had torn up fences, piled them on top of Souther's Hill, and built a bonfire to guide the rescuers back to shore.

As Joshua and his crew neared land, one wave, larger than the others, hoisted the boat and shattered it against a huge boulder. Crew and passengers were thrown into the violent waters. But the townspeople of Hull, heartened by Joshua's many victories, formed a human chain into the pounding breakers and picked up every person! The sea subsided, exhausted and defeated.

Another lifeboat was launched, and Joshua and the crew pulled to the *Bertha Walker*. By four in the morning seven more lives had been saved.

The ocean went insane. It had been denied too long. Ripping the last ship, the *H. C. Higginson,* from its cables, the raging sea hurled it into a death trap between two crags. Five men still clung to what was left of the *Higginson's* rigging. Crews from two other lifesaving stations had already tried to reach the ship with a Hunt gun, but they had failed.

"You'll never get a boat through that water," the rescuers warned Joshua. And it seemed they were right. Twice he and his crew launched the boat — twice they were hammered back to the beach. Now a gaping hole had been battered in the side of the lifeboat. Joshua's eyes narrowed with resolution.

"Make the repairs," he ordered.

As they were readying the boat for launching again, Joshua spotted an area on the beach where the waves were not quite so high. Had the ocean been careless? He and his crew hauled the boat there and launched it.

An hour later they took all five survivors back to shore.

Twenty-four hours had passed. Joshua and his crew had rescued twenty-nine people from four ships — a record unmatched in the history of lifesaving.

In 1889 the United States Life-Saving Service built a station in Hull. The law had decreed that the keeper of the station could be no more than forty-five years old. Though Joshua was sixty-two, the years rode lightly on his shoulders. In view of his exceptional record, the government changed the law and appointed him to the position.

During the next twelve years the struggle between Joshua and the ocean continued. While he was in charge of the station, he and his crew saved more than 500 human lives. During his entire career, he saved a total of more than 600 persons!

When interviewed after one heavy storm, Joshua said, "We saved all who were alive when we set out for them." It was then that folks remembered the oath that he had taken as a boy — his challenge to the sea.

One morning Joshua called a special drill. He had waited until a northeast gale arose. At seven o'clock he put his crew through their paces. Despite the pounding sea, the crew did well. Joshua himself took the most difficult position — the steering oar.

After an hour of exercises, he ordered his crew to return to shore. As the boat was pulled up onto the sand, Joshua looked out over the waters where his mother and tiny sister had gone down on the *Hepzibah* sixty-five years before.

He had kept his promise. He had avenged their deaths. "The tide is ebbing," he was heard to murmur. At that moment, the waters fell silent and the gale stopped. Joshua fell dead upon the sand. He had won his lifelong battle with the sea.